This book belongs to:

....

....

Quarto is the authority on a wide range of topics.

Quarto educates, entertains and enriches the lives of our readers—enthusiasts and lovers of hands-on living.

www.quartoknows.com

Author: Saviour Pirotta
Illustrator: Laura Wood
Designer: Victoria Kimonidou
Editor: Ellie Brough

Part of The Quarto Group
The Old Brewery
6 Blundell Street
London N7 9BH

A catalogue record for this book is available from the British Library.

ISBN 978 1 78493 813 0

Printed in China

Puss in Boots

Written by Saviour Pirotta

Illustrated by Laura Wood

Once there was a miller with three sons.

When the miller died, he
left his eldest son his mill.

His second son
his donkey.

And his youngest son, Bob...

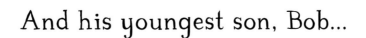

...his **cat.**

"How will a cat help me earn a living?" sighed Bob.

"Give me a bag and a pair of boots," said the cat, "and I'll show you what my cunning and imagination can do."

Bob was so surprised to hear a
cat talk, that he did as he was asked.

The cat caught a wild
rabbit with the bag.

He gave it to the
king as a gift.

The next day he
gave the king
two partridges.

"Who is sending me these wonderful gifts?" asked the king.

"My master, the Lord of Carabas Castle," replied the cat.

The next morning, the cat took Bob to the river.
"Take off your clothes and swim in the river," he said.

"But it's freezing,"
complained Bob.

"Do as I say, and you'll soon be a prince," said the cat.
"When you see a carriage, pretend you are drowning."

Soon, the king and his daughter drove past on their early morning ride.

"Help!" shouted Bob.

"Thieves stole my master's clothes and threw him in the river," said the cat to the king.

The king ordered his men to rescue Bob and to fetch fine clothes to replace his stolen ones.

Bob looked like a prince in his new clothes. The king's daughter had never seen a finer looking man.

The king invited Bob to
join them on the ride.

Soon the carriage came
to a castle on a hill.

"That is Castle Carabas,"
said the cat. "Your Majesty
is welcome to visit, but allow
me to run ahead and make
everything ready."

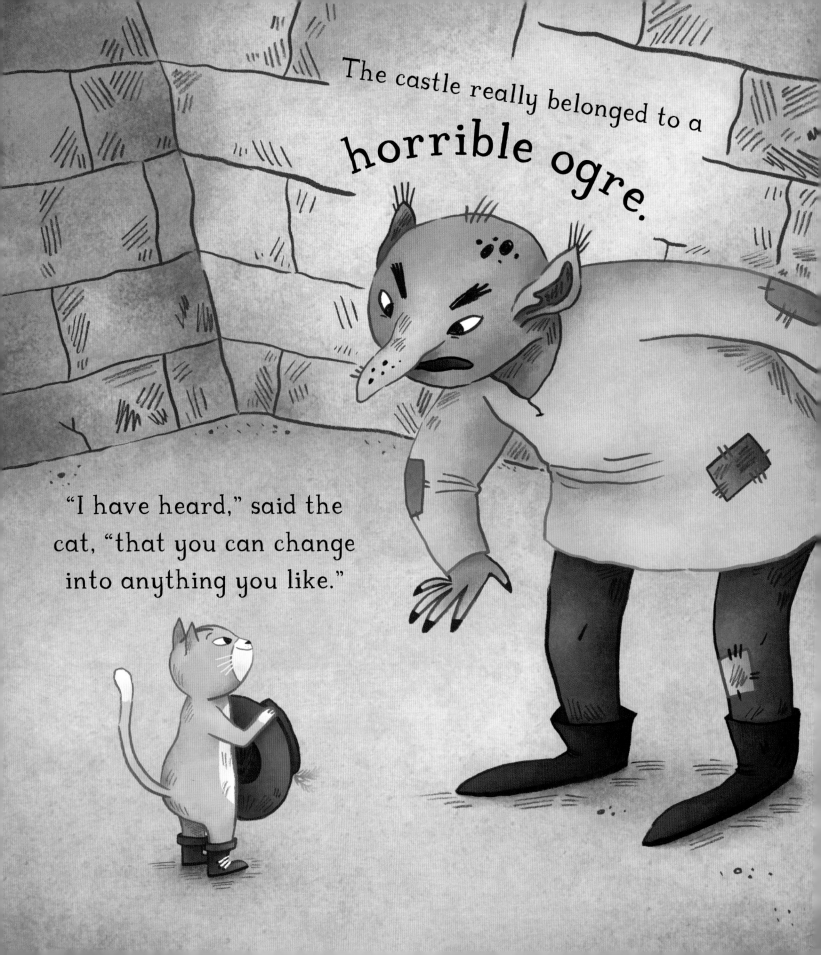

The castle really belonged to a **horrible ogre.**

"I have heard," said the cat, "that you can change into anything you like."

"You heard right," chuckled the ogre.
And he turned into a roaring tiger.

"Ah," said the cat. "But I bet you can't change into something tiny, like a mouse?"

The ogre **roarrrred** with laughter. "Can't I?"

The **roar** turned into a **squeak** as he changed into a mouse.

The cat pounced ...
... and gobbled him up!

The king's carriage arrived
and the cat welcomed them
to Carabas Castle.

The princess was now
in love with Bob, and the king
was very impressed with the castle.

Bob and the princess were married soon after.

"Thank you, Puss," whispered Bob.
"Your cunning and imagination have
helped me to become a prince."

LORD PUSS IN BOOTS

The king was so happy, he made the cat a lord.
Everyone called him **Puss in Boots.**

Next Steps

Discussion and Comprehension

Ask the children the following questions and discuss their answers:

• What did you like most about this story?

• What was the name of the son who was given the cat?

• Who did the cat trick? Can you say how?

• Do you think that the cat was a hero or a villain? Can you explain why?

• What would you think if a cat started talking to you?

Composing Sentences

Ask the children to look in the book and tell you the names of the characters in the order that they appear in the story. Write the names down using the correct punctuation, with capital letters for titles and check through the order with the children. Ask the children to draw a picture of each character and label with their names in a sentence, using the correct punctuation. For example: 'This is the donkey.'

Paint a Picture

Give the children a large sheet of paper and paints. Ask them to paint a picture of their favourite part of the story. On white paper ask them to write a title for the painting, for example 'Bob in the River' or 'The Ogre Turning into a Mouse'. To finish, stick the title on the painting.